THE WORLD IS IN DANGER!

An evil sorcerer ...
A mad king ...
A brave prophet ...
A wicked queen ...
Bloodthirsty soldiers ...

You can meet all kinds of people—from almost any country or century—when you travel in Professor Q's time machine. But now the insane historian, Dr. Zarnof, has captured the machine—and wants to use it for his own evil plot to rule the world!

Can you find him? Can you stop him?

What happens will depend on the choices you make. But one thing is always true: only by using your wits can you get safely back to the twentieth century....

There are over thirty possible endings to this story! And it all starts with how you handle a strange interruption at your birthday party....

DR. ZARNOF'S PLOT

DONNA FLETCHER CROW

Chariot Books
DAVID C. COOK PUBLISHING CO.

**For all the roleplayers
who adventure at our house**

Chariot Books is an imprint of David C. Cook Publishing Co.

David C. Cook Publishing Co., Elgin, Illinois 60120
David C. Cook Publishing Co., Weston, Ontario

DR. ZARNOF'S PLOT
© 1983 by Donna Fletcher Crow for the text and Thomas Gianni for
the illustrations

Cover illustration by Paul Turnbaugh

Printed in the United States of America
89 88 87 86 85   5 4 3 2

ISBN 0-89191-788-8
LC 83-72506

CAUTION!

This is not a normal book! If you read it straight through, it won't make sense.

Instead, you must start at page 1 and then turn to the pages where your choices lead you. Your first choice—how to handle a strange interruption at a party of yours—is one you may have made before. But after that, your decisions can lead you to other times and places—and if you're not careful, you'll never get back!

If you want to read this book, you must choose to **Turn to page 1.**

Today is your birthday. All your best friends are at your house for the evening, drinking soda pop and eating pizza and chocolate cake. Almost all your friends, that is. You can't figure out why Chris isn't here.

"Hey, come on," Andy says, "open your presents!"

"Yeah, well ...." You hesitate as you swallow a big mouthful of chocolate cake. "I thought maybe I'd wait for Chris."

At that moment Chris rushes into the room. His cheeks are flushed, his hair tousled, and his eyes frantic.

"The professor's machine's been stolen!" he yells.

You jump up, knocking over a bottle of soda pop, which Dana manages to catch just in time. "AL's gone? That's impossible!" you shout.

Everyone starts talking at once. "Who's Al?" "I don't know anyone named Al."

You turn to your friends. "AL is Professor Q's time machine. Chris and I didn't say anything about it before because we were afraid you'd think we were crazy, but we had some really great adventures. ..."*

Chris is tugging at your sleeve. "Come on, we've got to help the professor find it! The police can't help. They'd think he was nuts if he called and said his time machine had been stolen."

You look around the room. The rest of your friends are expecting a party.

"What are you waiting for?" Chris urges.

Choices: **You say, "I'm coming; anyone else want to go along and help?" (turn to page 2).**
You say, "This is my birthday, I want to open my presents first" (turn to page 4).

To read about these adventures, ask for *Professor Q's Mysterious Machine* at your bookstore.

You're glad Dana has decided to come with you and Chris to look for the time machine. Her long black hair flies behind her as you race down the street to the professor's house.

When you get there, your old friend Professor Quinten is sitting in a daze in the middle of his laboratory. His computer screens are flashing messages and his desk is covered with drawings and computations, but the corner of the room where AL should be is horribly empty.

"Maybe you just pushed AL's invisibility button and forgot about it," you suggest hopefully.

The professor doesn't even answer, just shakes his shaggy head on its long, thin neck.

"Well, are there any clues?" Dana asks.

But all the professor does is shake his head again.

Suddenly one of the computers makes a beeping noise and flashes more rapidly than before.

"I think it's trying to tell us something," Dana says.

"Of course!" you yell. "These computers would have modems—they would be able to talk to each other!"

Chris beats you to the typewriter keyboard and types the code for talking to AL

GO AHEAD appears on the screen. You've made contact!

"Ask him where he is!" you and Dana yell together.

LOCATION? Chris types.

ZAR … The answer starts to appear on your screen. Then there is a flash, and the screen goes dead.

"Try again," you urge.

Chris shakes his head, "They turned him off—or unplugged the modem."

Go to page 3.

You turn to the professor, whose eyes seem out of focus behind his heavy glasses. "Listen!" you yell, shaking him by the shoulders. "Do the letters Z-A-R mean anything to you?"

All at once the professor comes to life. "Zar?" he shrieks in his odd, high-pitched voice. "I should have guessed! Dr. Zarnof, the history professor! He heard me speak at the university, and—" The professor grips you tightly by the arm. "Zarnof will use time travel for his own power, not for scientific and historical study. He must be stopped!"

Choices: **You leave now for Dr. Zarnof's house (go to page 6).**

You want to question Professor Q more (go to page 10).

4

Chris looks disappointed at your reply. "OK, I'll go without you, then." He leaves.

You turn to your presents. You get some really neat things: a new sci-fi game, two records you've been wanting, a T-shirt with your picture on it, and a gift certificate for a Super Grubber Burger plus a Gigantic Titanic Banana Split (which has a model of a ship sinking in it) at your favorite fast-food place.

When all the gifts from your friends have been opened, there is still one package left, with no card to identify the giver.

You tear the paper off and are even more puzzled than before. It is a small, red-bound book entitled *The Despotic Imperative* by some Dr. Zachary Zarnof. You hold it out with a puzzled frown on your face. "Does someone think I'm gonna read this?"

Go to page 5.

Dana looks at it. "I've never heard of the book, but I've heard of Dr. Zarnof. He's a real history brain at the university."

"Like you?" you say to her.

She shrugs, "Well, it is my favorite hobby, besides karate."

You toss the book to a table and turn to your new game.

"Hey, look," Pat says, picking a piece of paper off the floor. "This fell out of the book."

You unfold the small piece of paper and squint at the messy writing. Then you figure out most of the words: "Happy Birthday," it reads. "I have an offer that will interest you. Come to 1815 College Boulevard. NOW."

Choices: You go (turn to page 14).
You don't go (turn to page 7).

You look up Zarnof's address in the phone book. He lives across town, near the university. As you are jogging down the sidewalk, Dana gasps, "Wait a minute. Don't you think we should have some kind of plan? We can't just go in and demand AL back."

Chris shrugs. "I thought we'd just sneak around and peek in windows and things—see what we can learn."

"Maybe we could pose as computer repairmen," you say.

"I have an idea," Dana suggests. "We could say we're university students doing a special project, and that we've come to interview him. I could keep him busy talking while you two looked around."

"University students?" you ask. "Don't we look a little young for that?"

"We could tell him we're accelerated students—took a lot of advanced placement classes. I have a cousin who did that—a real egghead," Chris says.

Choices: You decide to sneak around the house (turn to page 120).
You decide to pose as students (turn to page 115).

Todd and Andy start reading the directions to the new game you just opened, and Pat and Kim turn their attention to the popcorn machine. But you can't get that mysterious message from Dr. Zarnof out of your mind.

"What do you melt the butter in?" Pat asks.

You get out a small pan, put some butter in it and set it on the stove, wondering what the note could have meant. You're beginning to think that it has something to do with AL. Suddenly, a curl of black smoke rises from the pan, and you smell something awful. "Oh, no! The butter!" you yell.

"Hey, what are you doing? Daydreaming?" Dana asks, taking the pan out of your incompetent hands.

"Listen, you guys carry on here," you say. "I'll be back later."

Once you have made the decision to follow up on that message you feel better. You jog to the address on the note.

Choices: You ring the doorbell (go to page 16).
You sneak around and look in the window (go to page 25).

In reply, the professor steps inside the cone and pushes a small red button on the side of the computer panel. The computer equipment disappears and it looks as if the professor is standing in an empty room with you.

"Come on, let's go!" Chris urges. "I don't care if all time does exist at once. I don't want to waste any!"

"Does the computer work like AL's?" you ask.

The professor nods proudly, "Only even more efficiently, of course," he adds. "Just a minute, don't forget these." Professor Q hands you the instant language converters you used on your earlier adventure in AL. Fortunately he has one for Dana, too. "Now, you'll be able to talk to anyone you meet in their own language. And they can talk to you."

The three of you are quickly strapped inside, Chris at the control board. "Well," he asks. "Where to?"

"Do you think AN's modem can locate AL if he's in space?" Dana asks.

"Or maybe we should take Dr. Z with us for a little extra information," you muse.

"Kidnap him?" Chris asks, sounding alarmed.

Choices: You get into time randomly (go to page 12).

Professor Quinten's horror finally jars him out of his stupor into action. "I wasn't ready to reveal this yet," he says, jumping to his feet, "but this leaves me no choice."

You follow him to a room you've never been in before—another workroom behind his main laboratory. In the center of the room is an object that looks like a huge glass cone balanced on its point. Four seats are suspended on swivels in front of a computer display resembling AL's. On the top is a glass ball with tubes running through it.

"What is it?" all three of you ask at once.

"This is AN5002. Recent research has revealed new facts about time. I have put these to work in a more sophisticated time machine."

"Better than AL?" Chris asks. "How?"

Go to page 11.

"Tachions, tachions!" the professor shouts, flapping his arms about and looking like a great white bird in his lab coat. "I've harnessed tachions!"

"Tachions," Dana says calmly. "Aren't those the particles that move backwards in time?"

"Precisely," says the professor, obviously recognizing a kindred spirit in Dana.

"Why is she shaped so funny?" you ask, running your hand over AN's smooth surface.

"New developments, new developments," chants the professor. "New understandings, new understandings—it's so enthralling!"

"That's great!" Chris says. "But can we go?"

"If AL is going into time, then it will be necessary," the professor says. "But I haven't tried her out yet. I only completed her yesterday."

"Does AN have an invisibility factor like AL?" you ask.

Turn to page 8.

"Sagebrush?" you yell when you step out of AN.

"I didn't know they had sagebrush in the Middle East," Dana says.

You hear a horse whinny. Looking in the direction of the sound, you see a swirl of dust—and above the dust a dark-haired rider wearing a bright feather head-dress.

"Where are we?" you yell, dashing back to Chris, who is still at AN's control panel.

"Er—I can't really tell where we are, but either I'm a bad driver or the chronograph is malfunctioning."

"Malfunctioning? What do you mean?" Dana demands, coming up behind you.

"Well, it says June 25, 1876," Chris says.

You glimpse a look of horror on Dana's face as you turn to look at a larger cloud of dust filling the horizon just over the hill. The earth trembles with the pounding of hundreds of hooves. A bugle blast rips a cavalry charge through the air.

"We're going to be all right!" you yell, feeling relief flood through you. "It's the cavalry!" You start to run toward them.

But Dana's voice is louder than the thundering hooves. "Stop! That's Custer! We're at Little Big Horn!"

From behind you hear an Indian war whoop. This looks like **THE END.**

"Want me to go along?" Dana offers.

"Might as well," you shrug. "If he wants to talk about history, you can translate for me. You guys go ahead and start the game," you say to your friends. "But don't eat all the pizza. We won't be gone long."

You were wrong.

"... And then after Alexander came the age of the Caesars..." You barely suppress a yawn as the short, fat Dr. Zarnof waves a pudgy finger in the air to emphasize a point he's making. You feel like he's been lecturing on ancient history for hours, and you can't imagine why he's telling you all this, or why those two thugs who ushered you in here would care about such things either.

Suddenly you blink and jerk forward in your chair, "Did you say *time machine*!" you almost yell.

"Haven't you heard a thing I've said?" he asks, obviously annoyed. "You are to be my pilot, just to get me there. With my superior knowledge of history, I can handle the rest!"

"The rest?" you ask weakly.

"I'll become the most important man in every kingdom—first minister—more powerful and richer than any emperor I serve. I'll virtually take over for King David. I'll be a Caesar! I'll rule the world with Alexander. And I won't make the mistakes they made—because I know all about it!"

Dana looks as dazed as you feel.

Choices: You jump up and boldly say, "So you stole Professor Q's machine!" (go to page 74).

You slyly ask, "How did you know I was a time machine pilot?" (go to page 19).

The door is answered by a grubby man in a dirty sweat shirt. "I, uh, think I have a book of yours," you stammer, holding out the small red volume.

He grabs the book and examines it. "Oh, yeah. The Doc wrote that. Well, he's busy now; I'll give it to him later. Thanks, kid."

As he shuts the door in your face, you hear a muffled scream that sounds like Chris. At the same time, someone from another part of the house shouts, "Hey, Joe!" The man shuts the door hastily, but you don't hear him lock it. You give him a few seconds, hoping he's Joe, then cautiously open the door and slip across the room in the direction the cry came from.

You peek in the half-open door and see a short fat man in a toga with laurel leaves wound around his shiny bald head. He looks like an ancient Roman, except that he's waving a gun at your friend. "You will take me to Rome, I tell you!"

You jump the Roman gunslinger from behind. You have the advantage of surprise, so you easily knock the gun out of the pudgy hand. The bearded thug, Joe, peeks in, but when he sees who has the gun he takes off out the front door.

You sit on the rotund stomach while Chris wraps his belt around his assailant's wrists. "This is Dr. Zarnof," he says. "He had some crazy idea of being another Caesar or something, but he needed a pilot. You search for AL, and I'll take this guy to the police."

Go to page 20.

The window is too high for you to look in, so you search around for something to stand on. You're happy to find a wooden box by the back door. When you stand it up on end you are just able to peer in.

Three men are sitting around a table. One of them is wearing a white lab coat—probably Dr. Z. The other two are dressed in jeans, sweat shirts, and dirty sneakers—definitely not your idea of college professors.

They seem to be having some kind of argument. One man hits the table with his fist, then the other one jumps up and yells something at him. Dr. Zarnof looks worried. Unfortunately, you can't hear what they're saying.

One of the men starts to turn toward the window. You jump down quickly.

Go to page 21.

You are thinking frantically. You know the metal thing you bumped into is AL with his invisibility screen turned on. You're trying to decide whether you should try to make a dash for AL or for the door.

You don't get a chance to decide. "The Doc here don't like snoops, see," the thug with the shaggy beard says, pushing his face into yours.

The other one grabs your arm with a bruising grip, "And I don't see no football down here, kid." He hustles you out of the room and up the stairs.

Just before he shoves you out the front door he snarls, "You get off easy this time. But if I ever see you pokin' your nose in around here again you won't have no nose left to poke anywhere. Got it?"

You got it.

As soon as the door bangs shut, Chris and Dana run up and help you to your feet. "What happened?" they want to know.

"Well, I know where AL is," you say, "but we need help getting him back. Let's go talk to Professor Q."

Go to page 10.

"I knew you were a time machine pilot because that fool of a professor delivered a paper on your experiences to the university faculty. Only the others were greater fools than he was—they didn't believe him! I knew he was capable of inventing the machine, but not capable of making good use of it. I shall do that!"

Dr. Z jumps to his feet and begins pacing around the room, gesturing wildly, telling of the power that will be his.

Doctor Zarnof stops pacing as suddenly as he started. He stands right in front of you and looks at you sharply with his bright eyes. "Riches! Glory! You shall share them! I'll make you first minister. The thugs who—er, borrowed the machine for me aren't capable of assisting a leader of my potential, but I can see that you have real possibilities."

Choices: You think riches and glory sound good (turn to page 23).

You think Zarnof is crazy enough to be dangerous (turn to page 54).

You slip quietly down the stairs to Dr. Zarnof's basement, hoping you won't run into anyone like Joe along the way. The room is dark and seems to be full of odd-shaped objects. You grope around, longing to feel AL's smooth surface.

All of a sudden you freeze. Someone else is in the room. You are trying desperately to try to think of a plan when a familiar voice says, "Hey, birthday kid, is that you?"

"Dana! What are you doing here?" you whisper back, weak with relief.

"Finding AL, I think," she says. "But he doesn't seem to be in very good condition."

"What do you mean?" you cry.

You soon find out. Those funny shapes you were feeling were pieces of AL—disassembled.

"Looks like Dr. Z went berserk trying to figure out how to operate him," Dana says.

"Well, let's get him back to the professor," you say.

The professor is horrified at first to see his masterpiece reduced to a pile of rubble, but finally he pulls himself together.

"You know, this really shouldn't take too long to rebuild," he says, beginning to sound cheerful again. "Might even be able to do it tonight if I work all night. You kids want to help?"

Choices: You stay and help rebuild AL (go to page 28).

You return to your party (go to page 51).

On your hands and knees, you crawl quietly to the window well and peer down into the semidarkness. What you see looks promising. The dim light you saw is coming from a tv screen—a tv hooked up to a computer. You've at least located Zarnof's computer center—if only AL is nearby.

Then a terrible thought strikes you. What if Dr. Zarnof has AL's invisibility button turned on? How can you possibly locate something you can't see?

Go to page 37.

"We wouldn't have to get violent to get Zarnof to go with us," you explain. "He thinks we're reporters. We can tell him we've found something interesting, and would like his expert opinion."

Dana nods. "Just flatter him a little—that will do it."

It does. The professor hauls AN in his old pickup truck to a vacant lot near Dr. Z's lab, and you coax Doctor Zarnof over to see her.

"Most interesting," Dr. Z says, trying to sound unimpressed. "Not as advanced as my discovery, of course," he adds, clearing his throat.

"Get in," Dana urges. "Then you can explain it to us."

But once inside, it's you who do the explaining. "Dr. Zarnof, we know you have stolen Professor Q's time machine. This is a more sophisticated machine he has just designed. Now, do you want to go with us to find your men in AL or would you have us all stay here and expose you?" You are pleased at the steadiness and mastery of your own voice.

Dr. Z's round head is glistening with perspiration. "I ... er ... ah ... you can't prove anything," he stammers.

"Oh, yes we can," you retort.

Dr. Z hangs his head dejectedly.

"Where were your men going in AL?" Chris demands.

"I don't know. That didn't matter. I just wanted them to check out how it worked. I do know one of them said he wanted to see some beautiful women." Dr. Zarnof takes a grubby handkerchief out of his pocket and wipes his head.

"There were a lot of beautiful women in the Bible," you say.

"Jezebel?" says Dana.

"Yes, that's one name I suggested," says Zarnof.

Jezebel is on page 30.

You don't really trust Dr. Zarnof, but he might be able to get you into some important places. Besides, you tell yourself, you really hold the upper hand, because you are the one who knows how to fly AL.

"It's a deal, partner," you say, "but Dana goes, too."

The doctor looks doubtful and begins to hedge. "Well, of course I'd be delighted to have the young lady in my court. But there are only two seats in the machine."

"I've thought of that," you say, looking at a small chair at a desk across the room. "Got a screwdriver?"

Dr. Z goes for a screwdriver with no more argument. "Are you game?" you ask Dana.

"Why not?" she says. "I'd love to meet some of those people. And you can always bring us back, can't you?"

"No problem," you assure her as the doctor returns and leads you down a flight of stairs.

"AL! Good to see you!" You greet your old friend and run your hand over his wavy, egg-shaped surface.

You send Dr. Z off to get one of his belts to make a seat belt for Dana, and tell Dana to rummage around in the closet and see if she can find anything to make costumes from. "Rummage!" sniffs the doctor, returning with a belt. "Don't insult me! I have prepared a complete wardrobe. You may share some of yours with your friend."

Turn to next page.

You look inside AL and see the space under the control panel jammed with richly embroidered robes, sandals, headpieces, and of course, translator boxes. "Pretty sure of yourself, aren't you?" you say with grudging admiration.

"I always expect to succeed," Zarnof replies.

"Where to, boss?" you ask when everyone is robed and buckled in.

"I think we should give King David and the nation of Israel the benefit of my superior knowledge first," says Dr. Zarnof.

"Any particular time?" you ask.

"Well," Dana blurts out, "if you want to get in good with David, you might show up before he's king, when he's running from Saul and needs help."

The doctor doesn't argue, so you set the gauges according to Dana's instructions.

Go to page 26.

The backyard is dark, and you feel jumpy—for good reason. You're crawling on your hands and knees toward a lighted window when you see another light: a flashlight, held in the hands of a policeman.

"I was patrolling down the street, and I thought I saw somebody creeping around back here!" he exclaims. "There's been a lot of vandalism in town these days, kid. I suppose you have a good reason for sneaking around private property in the middle of the night?"

"Well, um … uh …" you stammer. You do have a good explanation: that note from Dr. Zarnof, plus your knowledge that Professor Q's time machine is missing.

But you're not sure it will sound so good down at the police station.....

THE END

David and his men are camped in the desert wilderness of Jeshimon. You land on a small plateau. It is protected on one side by steep, yellow hills honeycombed with caves. On the other side the land falls away in a sheer drop to the valley hundreds of feet below. You're glad you got there in AL. You'd hate to climb or ride a donkey up the steep trails.

Dana is surveying the many cave openings. "I wonder how we find a vacant room in this motel," she says.

Zarnof gives a jeering laugh. "I don't plan to stay here long enough to worry about it. As soon as I get David crowned king, I'll be moving into quarters more suitable for royalty."

You start to remind him that you're partners, but you are interrupted by a sharp warning cry from a sentry.

Across the deep, narrow valley there is a slight movement. It looks like an ant colony forming. The word spreads quickly—Saul is coming to battle David. David has a few hundred men. Saul has several thousand.

**Choices: You stay with David (go to page 41).
You think you'll be safer in Saul's camp (go to page 34).**

It doesn't take long for the three of you to have AL in working order again. The professor asks you and Dana if you want to go for an adventure—as his way of saying thanks. You sure do!

"We've been studying John Mark in Sunday school," you say to Dana as you each tuck your translator boxes inside your loose, homespun robes. "How about visiting him? Let's see. He started out in Jerusalem. Then he went to Antioch, and from there on some journeys...."

"I'm game for anything!" Dana grins with excitement.

Choices: You go to Jerusalem to see what it's like (turn to page 35).
You think journeys sound exciting (turn to page 91).

"Time machine pilot, eh? What if we don't believe in time machines?" the other thug snarls, spinning you around to face him.

You are saved having to reply by the appearance of a short, fat, bald-headed man in a white lab coat. In a nasal voice, he asks, "Did the kid say time machine, Joe?"

"Yeah, Doc. Ya want I should, uh, deal with this little problem?"

"Never mind, Joe, I'll see to that," Dr. Zarnof says, turning and looking at you sharply. "Suppose you tell me how you came by this 'time machine pilot' experience," he probes.

You speak slowly to keep your voice steady. "I piloted AL for Professor Q. Took the machine on its first voyage with a friend of mine. I know all about how it works."

"And why are you telling me this?" the doctor is still staring at you, his nose only a few inches from yours.

"Professor Q doesn't have the machine. He thinks you might." You decide to play greedy. "I don't care who has the machine. I just want to fly it."

The doctor steps back and rocks from his heels to his toes. "Hmmm. Well, it happens that I am in need of a pilot. You may fly the machine, with me as your passenger."

You gulp. You hadn't counted on that. But there doesn't seem to be any choice.

Go to page 32.

"Wow," Dana says. "Jezebel is beautiful all right!"

You are hidden behind some curtains in a pillared room richly hung with turquoise silk and cloth of gold. In the center of the room is a raised dais on which Queen Jezebel and King Ahab are reclining in a pile of ornately embroidered and tasseled cushions. A slave is kneeling to one side, pouring wine into golden goblets. Another slave stands behind them, waving a huge fan of feathers that must have come from a *very* large bird.

Jezebel has a rich olive skin, snapping black eyes, ruby red lips, and long, glossy black hair. She is wearing a finely draped white robe embellished with gold threads, and a golden headdress.

One man in the room looks very much out of place. He wears a coarse black wool mantle over a robe of rough camel's hair. His thick brown beard is shaggy and he carries a rude wooden staff.

But when he speaks, he commands total attention. He points at Ahab and Jezebel and announces, "You have ordered our people to worship your false god Baal. Now the Lord God Jehovah says there shall be no dew or rain in your land until he allows it."

The man turns sharply and strides out the door.

Jezebel, who had been stunned into momentary silence, leans forward and calls, "Elijah, wait!"

But the prophet has gone.

Choices: You follow Elijah (go to page 33).
You stay in Ahab's court (go to page 110).

You turn back to the corner that had looked so innocently empty, and feel carefully for AL's invisibility button. As soon as your old friend is visible again, you and the doctor put on the ancient-looking robes and translation equipment Professor Q had made, and climb inside. You explain that AL flies both in space and in time, and that you can choose your destination from the choices offered on his cartograph and chronograph screens.

The doctor looks at the dates flipping by on the chronograph. "One thousand B.C. Try that," he orders.

You nod and turn on the cartograph map. Each time you push a key the screen shows a more detailed map of a selected area. Finally Dr. Zarnof points a chubby finger at the screen. "Take me to Philistia—that ought to be as good a place as any to start."

"Start what?" you ask.

He turns and smiles wickedly. "My conquest of history."

Choices: You tell AL to do as Dr. Zarnof says (go to page 38).

You have an idea of your own (turn to page 47).

You follow Elijah eastward across the land until he comes to a small brook.

"There aren't any beautiful women around here. I don't think we're going to find AL in this wilderness," Chris observes.

"I don't see *anything*," Dana says. "It's a good thing I've still got some Granola bars in my purse."

"That's not all we need," you say. "We forgot to change our clothes. We still have blue jeans on!"

"Uh-oh," Chris says. "Do you suppose we could make something out of animal skins? That's what Elijah did."

Dana shudders, but you do find some animal skins that have been picked clean by vultures and tanned in the sun. They are scratchy, but less conspicuous than what you had been wearing before. Dr. Z can't find anything large enough to cover his enormous girth, so Dana suggests he rip the sleeves out of his lab coat and drape it like a toga.

It is now evening and you are ravenous. You begin to wonder what Elijah plans to do for food. Suddenly a flock of large black birds flies over, each carrying something in its beak. Watching from a distance, you see him hold out his hand. The birds place chunks of bread and meat right in it!

The flock is large, so you try it, too. But the ravens don't drop anything in your hands. So you each eat half a Granola bar and save the rest for later.

"These skins are awfully uncomfortable," Dana says. "Why don't we fly back to the professor's and get some robes? Maybe AL's turned up in the meantime."

"I'd hate to miss anything here, though," Chris says.

Choices: You fly back to the professor's for new robes (go to page 84).

You stay with Elijah (go to page 40).

The valley is so narrow a man could shout across the gorge, but it takes six miles of treacherous, roundabout trails to go from one side to the other. You carefully creep down the precipitous mountain, unseen by David's sentries. Dana is in excellent shape from her karate training, but Dr. Z is soon huffing and puffing loudly from the exertion of the climb.

It is easy enough to slip across the narrow valley, keeping to the shadows and avoiding rocks and pit-falls. But when you start to climb the hillside on which Saul's army is encamped, disaster strikes.

Zarnof trips on the root of a low-growing shrub and falls with a loud "Oooph!" Saul's sentries grab you roughly, mutter about enemy spies, and drag you off. Every time Zarnof yells, "But we've come to help you!" you get another jab with the spear tip.

But then, your mother didn't say life would always be fair.

THE END

You land in an olive grove on a hillside outside Jerusalem, and push AL's invisibility button.

"What a beautiful city!" Dana exclaims. "Look at all the white buildings gleaming in the sun!" She turns, then points to a magnificent structure on top of a hill. "That must be Herod's Temple. I can't believe we're really here! But how do we find Mark?"

"Well," you say, "I know that his mother's name was Mary, and that they have a large home that the Christians met in. That's a start, anyway."

The two of you wind through the narrow, cobbled streets of the city, knocking on doors of large homes asking for Mary and John Mark. When you find what you're looking for, you realize that you're part of quite a crowd. From what others are saying around you, large numbers of Christians gather here for meals and for worship services. And Peter, the apostle, apparently comes here often to teach.

As you and Dana join in on some of the cleaning, serving, and other community chores, you begin to notice that some of the so-called Christians there never join in on the prayers or teaching or worship. They just show up at mealtime. They don't even help with the work!

One day, as you're carrying a serving bowl, you notice a couple approaching you. This man and wife really irritate you. They always seem to complain and never to help. You think they're just claiming to be Christians to get free meals.

Choices: You go ahead and give them food (turn to page 42).
page 42).
You turn and give the food to someone else (turn to page 48).

Before you see Samson, you hear the mocking shouts and jeers of the people. Then he is led before you—a man of gigantic proportions, muscles rippling under his bare skin. He wears only chains and a coarse tunic from his waist to his knees. His skin has become pale white from his time in prison. Where his eyes once were you see nothing but scars.

He is taken into the center of the courtyard of the temple, where the crowd makes him leap and dance while they laugh at him.

Finally, one of the rulers says, "Enough. Take the prisoner away now." You feel so sorry for this Samson. You see a servant boy approach him to lead him away.

Choices: **You run ahead of the servant boy and take Samson's hand yourself (turn to page 44).**
You don't want these Philistines to see how you feel about Samson, so you turn away and look for Dr. Zarnof (turn to page 85).

Fortunately the basement window is easily pried open. You drop to the floor soundlessly and look around you. Well, you can see that AL isn't sitting out in the open in this room. Suddenly you hear voices coming downstairs. You make a dash for the only hiding place you see—a pile of boxes in the corner—as the door opens.

But you don't make it. Your head strikes a hard metal object, and you fall to your knees. The room is spinning around.

The next minute you are dragged roughly to your feet by a burly man who looks like he needs a shave and smells like he needs a bath. "All right, kid, what's the big idea?" he growls.

Choices: **You say, "I'm a time machine pilot, and I hear you might have a job opening" (go to page 29).**
You say, "We were playing catch and I think my football rolled in here" (go to page 18).

When the time machine lands, you look around, trying to figure out where you are. You know AL was only programmed to travel to the Middle East, because of Professor Q's interest in the Bible. But you're pretty sure these people aren't Israelites.

A group of people hurry by, laughing and merry-making, and enter a large and elaborate building just behind you. From every direction, crowds of people are streaming in. They all seem to be celebrating.

"A celebration is an excellent place to make my move," Dr. Zarnof says as he starts toward the crowd. You think you'd better go, too.

Once inside, you realize that the building is enormous. You figure that there are several thousand people inside, and more are looking in on the center courtyard from the roof, which is supported by great marble columns.

In the center of the building is a statue on a high pedestal. The people are dancing around it, bowing, and laying flowers and fruit at its base. The idol has the body of a fish, but the head and arms of a man. He has long hair and a beard, and wears a tall, rounded helmet.

The dancing people begin to shout: "Our god Dagon has delivered our enemy into our hands! Call Samson out, so that he can entertain us."

Go to page 36.

"I sure didn't sleep well," you say the next morning, stretching your aching muscles.

"Well, here comes Elijah's breakfast," Dana says as a flock of ravens flies over with meat and bread again. You eat the other half of your Granola bar.

Dr. Z is looking even more uncomfortable than you feel. "Well, doctor, what do you think of time travel now?" you ask.

"Look, kids, if I knew where AL was I'd tell you," he snaps. "I can't take much more of this."

"I'm not sure any of us can," Chris says. "How about moving up just a little bit in time till the drought's over?"

"Or until the drought's *almost* over," Dana suggests. "I'll bet Elijah and Ahab do some interesting bargaining then."

Choices: You agree with Dana (turn to page 43).
You just want the drought to be over (turn to page 86).

The women of David's camp begin walking among the men, serving the evening meal—big bowls of a tasty, spicy porridge. You realize it may be the last meal before a battle. Then everyone lies down to get some rest.

You can't sleep very well on the hard ground, so you wake easily at the sound of voices.

It's dark. David is standing in the middle of the camp, talking with two of his men. "Who will go down with me to Saul's camp?" he asks.

"I will," one replies.

"Thank you, Abishai," David says.

You realize you aren't the only one awake. As soon as David and Abishai are gone, Zarnof jerks his head in their direction, and you and Dana follow quietly.

It's rough going. There is no moon, but the starlight shows the general shape of the land. You have to rely on caution and instinct to get you quietly over the stony, treacherous ground.

Go to page 116.

Grudgingly you ladle out a scoop of cooked meal and thrust the bowl into the woman's clawlike hands. You are spared having to give food to her husband because your serving pot is empty. As you turn to go to the kitchen for a refill, you see John Mark. He is startled by the look of anger in your face as you approach him. "What is it, my friend? You are troubled."

"Why do you let people like that sponge off the rest of you?" you growl, jerking your head at the people you have just left. "They never work; they never worship; they just eat and gripe!"

Mark, who is not much older than you are, puts his hand on your shoulder and takes you a little way apart from the others in the room. "We can't judge what's in another man's heart," he says. "Besides, many who come only for the food will learn of Christ's death for them and become true believers."

You nod slowly. "But how can your mother afford all this hospitality?" you ask.

Before Mark can reply, a man named Barnabas comes in with a bag of money, which he gives to Peter.

"What is this, Barnabas?" Peter asks.

Go to page 50.

"Look how brown everything is!" Dana says when you get out again.

"It looks like Elijah got the drought he promised," you say. "How much of a time jump have we made?"

Chris checks his instruments. "Three and a half years," he says.

"Three and a half years with no rain!" you say.

"Look! Isn't that Elijah?" Dana says as a tall, gaunt figure walks into view over a little hill in front of you.

"Who's that man on horseback riding up to him?" Chris asks.

"It looks like King Ahab," you say in surprise.

You flip AN's invisibility button and walk up to the guards and shepherds surrounding Ahab.

"Elijah! Is it you—the one who has caused Israel so much trouble?" the king challenges him.

"No," Elijah replies calmly, his forceful voice ringing on the desert air. "It is not *I* who brought drought and famine to Israel. It is *you*, because you have broken God's commandments and worshiped Baal."

You draw back, wondering how the king will take such brave words, but Ahab is silent.

Elijah continues, "Send for the prophets of Baal—all 450 of them—and the leaders of Israel. Then meet me on Mount Carmel."

"I wonder if that's the first time anyone ever gave orders to the king?" Dana says as Ahab rides off obediently.

At this, the usually silent Dr. Z laughs. "Not likely. I'll bet his majesty takes plenty of orders from that queen of his!"

"Come on," Dana says. "I want to see what happens."

Go to page 49.

44

You are amazed at the size of Samson's hand—it must be four times the size of yours. You lead him away from the center of action, surprised at your own impulse to be gentle with this strong man. But the crowd continues to shout.

"Here's Delilah—how about a little kiss?"

"Come on, Samson, show us your muscles!"

"Who's more powerful now—your God or ours?"

Each shout is followed by uproarious laughter.

Samson ignores it all and says to you, "Put me by the pillars that support the temple, so that I can lean on them."

You follow his directions and then move away. But as you leave, you hear Samson praying softly: "O Lord, remember me. Please strengthen me once more, so that I can have revenge on the Philistines." Then he puts those huge hands on the pillars beside him, one to his left and one to his right.

"Oh, no!" you murmur. You have just remembered from your own Bible reading what's going to happen next. You've got to get out of there!

Choices: You run out of the temple (turn to page 58).
You look around for Dr. Zarnof (turn to page 106).

46

You follow Dr. Zarnof, who is making his way down into Saul's camp from one direction, while David and Abishai are leaving in another. Apparently Zarnof wants to join Saul's army now, which isn't hard to do when they're all asleep.

You've just gotten seated, however, when the soldiers all wake up. David is on top of a far hill, calling out to the whole camp, chiding the men for sleeping while their king was in danger. He holds up the spear and water jug, and asks Saul to stop pursuing him.

The soldiers around you seem confused by all this, and King Saul seems ashamed. "I have sinned," he cries. "Come back, David, my son!"

David does not accept the invitation back into Saul's camp: apparently he still doesn't trust the king. "Let one of your young men come up here and get your spear and water jug back," he offers instead.

Saul motions a young soldier to go up the hillside.

Choices: **You follow the soldier up the hill, intending to stay with David once you get there (turn to page 68).**
You stay with Saul, since he doesn't seem like a bad king (turn to page 71).

"Keep your eye on those dials, and tell me if they go over midway to the right," you tell the doctor, hoping to take his mind off what you're doing.

In a moment AL registers that you've reached your destination. Dr. Zarnof yanks the door open and jumps out, expecting to be in a strange land. He finds himself in Professor Q's laboratory.

Professor Q is as surprised as the doctor. The two men stand blinking at each other nervously. You stride to the telephone and punch the emergency number. "Send a squad car to Professor Quinten's," you say, giving them the address. "We just nabbed a fellow trying to steal some of our lab equipment."

Soon the police have left with the crook. Professor Quinten is standing by AL, patting the machine as if it were a pet horse. Then he seems to remember that you are in the room.

"Oh, I say, er—thank you. I mean, how can I reward you? Would you like to take another trip or anything?"

Choices: You say, "Maybe another day, thanks. I'd like to get back to my birthday party" (turn to page 51).

You say, "We're studying John Mark in Sunday school. I'd like to go see him— with my friend Dana, the history nut" (turn to page 35).

With a disgusted look on your face, you turn your back on the freeloaders and scoop an extra portion for a little boy sitting with another group. You are about to scoop another bowl for his sister when you feel a strong hand grip your shoulder.

You turn and look up into the kindly brown eyes of Peter. "Why did you refuse food to those people?" he asks quietly, so the others won't hear.

"Because they don't deserve it," you answer hotly. "They aren't real Christians! They're just beggars and they're too lazy even to sit by the Temple gate and beg like proper beggars."

Peter looks at you sadly. "My friend, our Lord told us to feed his sheep."

"But that's just the point!" you say. "Those people aren't his."

Peter is quiet for a moment, but you are held by his eyes. "Then who has greater need of our food and our love than they do?" he asks.

You look at the bowl in your hands. You don't feel much like eating right now. You turn to give it to the hungry woman you refused earlier. But she isn't there.

THE END

Two altars are standing on the mountaintop, and Baal's prophets in their yellow robes are grouped around one.

Elijah strides forward, holds up his staff, and calls to the people in a thundering voice. "People of Israel! How long will you wander back and forth between the Lord God Jehovah and Baal? If Baal is god, worship him. If the Lord is God, worship him and him only. Today you must choose!" Elijah turns to the false prophets behind him. "All of Baal's prophets can prepare an offering, lay it on the wood, and pray to their god. I will pray to the Lord. The god who sends down fire to light the offering is the real God."

The people begin talking excitedly to each other. "That's a real test." "Who do you think will win?" "If Elijah loses, Ahab will kill him."

Go to page 60.

"I sold my land, and I want all the money to be used to help the followers of Jesus who are in need," Barnabas replies.

There is great rejoicing over Barnabas's gift and he is praised for his generosity. You would like to be a real part of all this. You and Dana look at each other. You don't have much of value with you, but you are each wearing a ring. Hers is set with a lime green stone. Yours is plain gold with your initials engraved inside.

Dana slips her ring off and hands it to you. "Give this to Peter for me," she says. "I've got ot get back to the kitchen."

Choices: You give both rings to Peter and explain that one is Dana's (go to page 57).
You decide to give Peter the rings and claim that both are yours (turn to page 55).

"About time you came back to your own party!" Randy says with a grin as you walk in.

"This is a great game," Kim says. "Want to play?"

"Pretty soon. I think I'll open my presents first," you say. You just have the wrapping off the biggest box when your doorbell rings. It is three more friends who have come to wish you a happy birthday.

They have all brought you presents, too. You break out a new batch of soda pop and plug in the popcorn popper.

More adventuring will have to wait until later.

THE END

With a swift movement you take the last earthenware jar and race down the hill. The others started ahead of you, but you easily catch up. When the jug is full of water, it is heavier. Uphill is also harder going, but your excitement gives you energy.

When you have emptied your water jars over the altar, wood, and sacrificial bull, Elijah commands you to fetch more. You're beginning to agree with the people who think this is rather strange, but you obey Elijah.

When he tells you to do it a third time, you wish you hadn't been in such a rush to be helpful. Your arms are aching. But finally, not only is the altar soaked, but the trench around it is full of water, like a moat.

You stand back, waiting to see what Elijah will do now. He simply steps forward and raises his arms to heaven. "O God of Abraham, Isaac, and Jacob, let all the people know that you are God in Israel!"

Everyone looks up into the sky—and suddenly, it happens. A ball of fire shoots down from the sky to the altar, and the soggy wood does not deter it. The leaping flames consume not only Elijah's sacrifice and the wood, but the very stones of the altar itself! You fall to your knees in amazement.

"The Lord is God! The Lord is God!" all the people are yelling. You recover and look for your friends—and see a second miracle. Dr. Zarnof is yelling "The Lord is God!" with the throng. The harsh sneer is gone from his face. He is radiant with joy.

THE END

"Uh, yeah, sure," you say, thinking fast. "Good plan. We'll, uh, be right back. I have to get my equipment—can't go flying off into time without my maps, charts, compasses, things like that."

Dr. Zarnof looks doubtful.

"You want to get lost out there and maybe not get back?" You press your advantage.

"All right, thirty minutes. No longer! If you aren't back by then, I'll send Joe and Mac after you."

"We read you, loud and clear," you say, heading steadily for the doorway that Dana has already exited through.

Once outside, you don't stop running until you're at the police station. You had expected to be laughed at, but the police captain listens intently to your story of robbery and attempted kidnapping.

Much to your surprise, however, you discover it isn't Dr. Zarnof the police are interested in. The captain pulls out a stack of mug shots and you easily identify Mac and Joe, Zarnof's accomplices.

"Well, this is your lucky day!" the policeman tells you. "There is a $500 reward for information leading to the arrest of these two."

Pretty good birthday present, eh?

THE END

As you approach the disciple with the rings, you think about how impressed he will be with your gift. Suddenly, you are elbowed aside by an important looking man in a yellow and purple robe who pours a heavy bag of coins out on the table.

"My wife and I have sold our land. We want to give all the money we made to help the church," he announces loudly.

Peter sits quietly for a moment, looking from the pile of coins to the man's eyes. You wonder why the man steps back.

Then Peter stands and speaks in a ringing voice that fills the room, "Ananias, your money was yours to do with as you pleased. Why do you pretend that you gave all of it, when you know that is not true? Don't you see? You are lying to God."

You gasp as Ananias falls down at your feet. He's dead. Several men carry his body away. You are still standing frozen to the spot when Ananias's wife, Sapphira, comes in.

Like her husband, she lies when Peter asks her about the money. The apostle points at her accusingly. "Sapphira, your husband is dead because he lied to God. You will pay the same penalty."

Instantly, Sapphira falls to the floor and dies. As she is carried out, John Mark speaks to you quietly. "In the days of King David, God told Samuel to look on a man's heart, not the outside. As you can see, holiness is important to God."

You nod weakly, thankful you did not have the chance to lie.

THE END

56

You follow David across the narrow valley again and up a hill. He raises his arms and begins to shout. At first you think he is giving a signal to his troops to attack Saul. Then, as you listen, you realize he is telling Saul's army what he has done.

"Abner, captain of Saul's troops! Are you a courageous man? Then why have you not protected your king? Someone came to destroy him, and I have proof. Look for the king's spear and the jug of water that were beside his head." The clear morning air carries David's voice, and the mountains amplify the sound like a public-address system.

Saul shouts back in reply, "Is that your voice, my son David?"

"Yes it is, my lord. Why do you pursue your servant this way? What have I done?" David calls across the valley.

Saul seems genuinely ashamed. "I have sinned," he replies. "Return to me, David. I will never again do you harm."

But David doesn't seem interested in the invitation down into Saul's camp. "Let one of your young men come up and get the spear and water jug," he suggests instead.

Choices: **You think David should trust the repentant Saul, and you go down to join Saul's troops (turn to page 71).**
You stay with David (turn to page 68).

You present both rings to Peter, explaining that one is Dana's. "God bless you, my children," he says. "It is good that you care more about others' needs than your own possessions."

You and Dana stay with Mary for some time. You enjoy the warm fellowship of the people and find it exciting to be learning about Jesus from the people who actually lived and worked with him. And there is so much to do! Mary and her servant girl, Rhoda, are busy long before the sun is up and long after it goes down caring for everyone. You help them all you can.

You have just finished scrubbing the kitchen walls one day when three Christians rush in with terrible news. James, one of the four fishermen who left their nets to follow Jesus, has just been put to death by Herod Agrippa.

Everyone is standing in stunned silence at this news when another believer comes in. "Have you heard?" he cries. "Peter has been arrested, and Herod has issued orders to execute him also!"

Even though Mark is one of the younger men there he assumes a place of authority in his mother's home. "We must pray for Peter," he says.

Most of the people follow Mark's lead, but one man says, "I'm not going to sit around here waiting to be arrested! I think I'm more useful to God alive than dead." He strides out.

Choices: You stay to pray (go to page 69).
You leave also (go to page 67).

As you run out of the temple, you look back over your shoulder. Samson is leaning on the pillars as if he's tired. The Philistines think that's funny, too—until he begins to push.

"Look out, it's crumbling!"

"His hair has grown back—his strength has returned!"

"AAAAAAaagh ...!"

You dive out of the temple doorway and roll into the street, barely escaping a huge stone block that just grazes your shoulder as it crashes to the ground.

You sit for a while, feeling the earth shake under you, and hearing the cries of the people inside. Then, finally, all is silent. No one inside survived, not even Samson.

You get up, brush yourself off, and walk slowly away. Even after you get back to AL, you are still frowning. You suppose those people deserved to die. It was God's judgment on them for mocking him. But you are worried about Dr. Zarnof. He wasn't exactly a nice guy, but should you have tried to rescue him?

THE END

As you hesitate, someone else moves up and takes the last jar. You're glad. It's really hot here on the mountaintop, and you've been standing in the middle of a mob of people for hours.

"I think I'll go sit down for a while," you say to your friends and move off to the side of the crowd. The only shady spot you can find is right up against the altar the prophets of Baal built. Everyone has moved over to watch Elijah, so it won't matter if you rest here for a few minutes.

You lean back against the shady altar and close your eyes to ease your aching head. You didn't sleep very well last night ....

You wake up as a rock smashes against the altar right next to your ear, and the cries of an angry mob reach your consciousness. "The prophets of Baal are false!" "They killed the prophets of God!" "They must die!" "Stone them!"

The prophets of Baal are cringing around their altar, and you can see no way to get out. A flying stick strikes you a fierce blow across the forehead. Everything begins to spin around in blackness. You sink to the ground.

Go to page 114.

60

The prophets of Baal begin to dance around their altar. At first their steps are lively, and their cries to Baal are clearly heard. But as the morning drags on, the priests in their yellow flapping garments become tired and desperate. Their dancing becomes hobbling, shuffling steps.

Elijah steps forward when the sun is straight overhead. "Call a little louder!" he mocks them. "Perhaps your god is busy or off on a journey. Perhaps he's asleep."

Straining their raspy voices, the priests shout louder and louder. In a last reckless act, they gash themselves with swords and spears as they dance, in the hope that Baal will see how desperate they are and take pity on them. The blood stains their robes and makes sticky blobs in the sand they trample. Still there is no answer from their god.

Then Elijah says to the crowd, "Come closer to me." You move forward with all the people. Elijah has dug a trench all around the altar in the hard, dry soil.

"Now fill four jars with water," Elijah orders.

Three people hurry forward and pick up the huge jars, then run down the hillside to a trickling stream to fill them.

You hesitate, wondering if this guy's crazy. Water, when he wants the sacrifice to burn?

Choices: You take the fourth jar to fill it with water (go to page 52).
You stay where you are (go to page 59).

Her flattery works, and you're shown into a little sitting room. "Well, what can you tell us about your work?" Dana asks. "We plan to send copies of this edition to several influential history foundations, so I know you'll want to give us a real scoop."

"Well, I'm not prepared to divulge the details as yet" Dr. Zarnof begins, "but I can tell you that I have a team of researchers who are about to go back in time." His beady eyes flash.

"Do you mean they're going tonight?" Dana asks, trying to keep any note of alarm out of her voice.

"That's right." Zarnof puffs out his chest like a pigeon. "You may have wondered about this lab coat I'm wearing. Not the usual attire for a historian, eh? But it is for one who's invented a time machine!"

Go to page 63.

"*You* invented it?" the three of you splutter at once. Zarnof doesn't answer. He is looking at his watch. "I really must go," he says. "Why don't you come back another time? Meanwhile, be quite sure to spell my name correctly in the headlines. That's Z-A-R-N-O-F," he says, pushing you toward the door.

As soon as the door is slammed shut, you all look at each other in horror. "AL is about to go somewhere in time," you moan. "Now we'll never get him back."

"Well," Chris says, "I guess there's nothing to do but go tell Professor Q the bad news."

"Wait a minute," Dana says. "I'd like to see if I could find out more of Zarnof's plans."

Choices: **You go back to the professor's (turn to page 10).**
You investigate the doctor more (turn to page 79).

"Now I wonder where we'll find Elijah," Chris says, surveying his cartograph. "He'll probably lead us to Jezebel."

"Type in 'Zarephath,'" Dana suggests.

You look at her, eyes wide in surprise.

"What's the matter?" she retorts. "You think I never went to Sunday school? I don't know if he's there now, of course, but I do remember a story about Elijah going there."

Shaking his head wonderingly, Chris sets the dials.

Dana is right. You are just walking into the village when you see Elijah talking to a woman there. She has handed him a drink of water from the jug she is carrying. "Please bring me a little food, too," he's saying, "for I am very hungry."

The woman looks at him in amazement. "Sir, I have no bread to give you. I am a poor widow. I have only a handful of meal and a little oil at home. I am picking up sticks to make a fire. Then I will bake one last bit of food for my son and myself before we die of hunger."

You look around. The drought Elijah foretold has come, and famine with it. Everywhere people are ragged and emaciated.

"Do not be afraid," Elijah says to her. "Do just as you planned, but first make a cake for me."

How can he ask that? you wonder. He is hungry, but this woman and her child are starving!

Choices: You grumble, "Surely he can find food somewhere else" (go to page 77).
You listen further (go to page 81).

You can see that David is troubled as he calls his followers around him. "Saul is the anointed king of Israel. The men in his army are our own people. Even though they have hunted us for years, it is not my will to do battle against them. Yet our treaty with Achish leaves us no choice but to march with him. We must call upon the Lord God to deliver us from this dilemma."

Then, with a look of great sadness, David leads his army out, falling in place behind other Philistine troops. You march all day. That evening, when you are making camp, you see a messenger approach David.

"Achish wishes to speak to you," the messenger says. David nods and follows. You follow David.

Achish's tent is hung with rich, embroidered tapestries. There are Persian carpets on the floor and plump cushions to lounge on. You get only one good glimpse before the flap is closed, but you can still hear the voices through the goatskin walls.

"My captains refuse to go into battle with you on their side," Achish says.

"Do you distrust me?" David asks.

"You know I don't," Achish replies. "I have always found you faithful. But my leaders cannot forget that you are an Israelite. They will not go into battle with you. Your troops must go back to Ziklag."

"I understand," David says.

When he emerges his face is radiant. His prayers have been answered.

THE END

"I'll just go have a word with David's commanders," Zarnof says, puffing out his already puffed chest. "When they hear my plan for joining forces with Saul against Achish, my true genius will be appreciated. Then I'll slip on ahead to Saul's camp to get everything ready. Meet me there," he orders as he strides off.

Dana waits until he's out of sight, then grabs your arm urgently. "It's time to get back to AL before something else happens," she says, and starts running toward the big boulder at the foot of the hill where you parked your time machine.

You don't stop to ask questions until you are safely inside AL. As you are buckling your seat belt, you suddenly have second thoughts. "Shouldn't we try to get Dr. Z, too?" you ask.

Dana shakes her head. "I don't think we can. I didn't know what he was planning to do, or I'd have tried to stop him sooner."

"Why?" you ask.

"I know how it ends. History is my thing, remember?"

"Oh, yeah," you say. "Well? Aren't you going to tell me?"

"I think I'll let you read it for yourself," she says, grinning mischievously.

"Read what?"

"I Samuel 29 and 31," she says tossing her long, dark hair.

"Are you serious? You aren't going to tell me?"

Dana laughs and shakes her head. "It's time you learned there are more ways to learn history than just flying a little egg around."

THE END

You figure that you'll be more useful to God alive and free than dead or in prison. God certainly didn't seem to protect every Christian: James had been killed, after all. You slip out into the street.

"What are we going to do now?" Dana asks you. "We don't know anybody we need to go warn or anything do we?"

You begin to feel uncomfortable. Maybe you should have had more confidence in prayer, and in God's control of the situation. You aren't sure. "Let's go to AL," you say slowly.

When you get back home, your friends are seated around a long table in your family room, deeply engrossed in the new game you got for your birthday. "Want to join our adventure group?" Randy invites.

"One of our leaders has been captured by the enemy," Kim says.

"We've heard that he's in prison," Todd continues.

"Any ideas?" the adjudicator asks.

"Maybe we should pray for him," you mumble.

Your friends all look at you strangely except Dana. She just nods. "We'll know better next time," she says.

THE END

Though Saul and his army depart, David does not trust the king's promise not to harm him. Yet he is tired of living in hiding. So David decides to go into Philistia, enemy territory, and convince them that he's joining their forces.

You don't think the plan will work, but it does. The ruler there, King Achish, even makes David governor of the town of Ziklag. His six hundred men and families settle there. You find living in a house a lot more comfortable than living in caves in the desert.

David's army spends its time raiding many of the ancient enemies of Israel nearby. Yet David convinces Achish that they have really been attacking Israel. Zarnof is pleased with David's skill in battle, with his cleverness in dealing with Achish—and most of all with the spoils of battle he himself is allowed to carry off. "Hardly needs my help at all. He'll make a great king—as long as he listens to my advice, that is."

But it is a precarious situation, and one day David finds himself in a real predicament. The Philistines are marching against King Saul's army! David now has to choose between making war on his own people and breaking his word to Achish, who has given him safe asylum and even a town.

Choices: You think David should break faith with the Philistine, Achish (turn to page 65). You think David should make war on his old enemy, Saul (turn to page 66).

The Christians begin praying. Some fall to their knees, some sit quietly, others stand with their arms extended toward heaven. Along with the rest, you ask God to do a miracle, to spare Peter from death in prison and bring him back to you.

Suddenly, in the middle of the prayer, you hear a loud knocking at the door of the outer gate.

"It's Herod's soldiers!" someone cries.

The young servant girl goes timidly to the door, opens the peephole, then scurries back. "It's Peter!" she exclaims.

"It's his ghost!" a woman shrieks. "Oh, Rhoda, you're imagining things," someone else says. "Quickly, everyone—go to the roof. Run! Be ready to escape down the vine to the orchard."

Choices: You think it's Roman soldiers (turn to page 78).
You think it's Peter (turn to page 76).

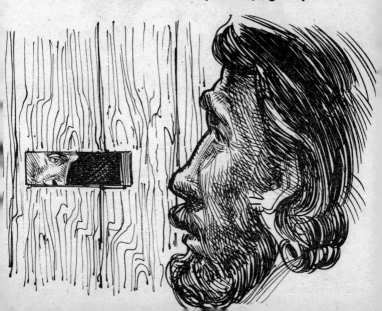

Along with the army, you return to Saul's home base of Gibeah. There's not much of a palace there—more like an army headquarters. But, with Zarnof in charge, you're soon in the center of what glory there is.

You're right about Saul, sort of. On his good days, he's a pretty good king. But he doesn't seem to worship the Lord anymore.

And he gets terribly moody. One day you happen to be in his throne room when something upsets him. *Zing!* A spear hits the wall near your shoulder. *Zing!* You hear another one coming.

This could be **THE END.**

As you look into the thin little face you see fear written there—and also hunger. "Did you take those because you're hungry?" you ask.

The tears that have been gathering in the child's eyes spill down the hollow cheeks as he nods.

"Are you a servant here?" Dana asks. He shakes his head. "What's your name?" she asks.

"Amos," he says in a choked little voice.

"Well, Amos," you say, "stealing isn't right even if you're hungry. Put the coins back. Then we'll arrange for you to earn some food."

You lead Amos to the lady that sent you for the water earlier, "This is my friend Amos. He wants to work for you. He's very good at, uh …" You look at him doubtfully; he doesn't look much good for anything. "Uh, carrying things," you finish hopefully.

"Oh, is he?" the woman says. "Well, it looks to me like he needs to carry some food to his mouth. Go tell the cook to give you a plateful, little one. Then we'll try you out carrying scraps to the pigs."

Amos doesn't say anything, but the look of gratitude he gives you is something you'll never forget.

Go to page 92.

Dawn is just breaking as you leave Mary's courtyard with Peter. Mark has chosen to go with Peter, too. The young man leads the way, slipping quickly through the olive grove and into a deserted street. You don't see anyone until you are nearly to the city gate. The gate is open, but guarded. You hold your breath, hoping there won't be trouble. Happily, your small party slips through unnoticed.

Once through the gate, Peter turns to you and places his big, rough hand on your shoulder. "I must leave," he says, "but I feel there is something you would like to ask me first. Is that not so?"

You nod, surprised at his insight. "I guess I don't understand something," you say. "Why did God go to all that bother—sending an angel and everything—to rescue you, when he let James be killed?"

Peter lowers his eyes, and suddenly you're sorry you asked such a delicate question.

"My child, I don't understand either," the fisherman admits. "I'm certainly not a better man than James was. All I know is that Jesus told us we would be persecuted. Now James is with the Lord. But my life was given back to me last night. So I think God would like me to serve him with it as long as I have it, don't you?"

You nod.

"This is also true of your life," Peter adds.

You'd never thought of that before. You've got a lot to ponder as you go back into Jerusalem to find Dana and AL.

THE END

74

"I didn't steal the machine: I borrowed it for the good of history. But we won't debate terms." Dr. Zarnof pulls a gun out of a small drawer in a table, "We're wasting time!" he shouts. "Down those stairs! You, too," he motions to Dana.

"But AL only has two seats," you protest, hoping to save your friend.

"We'll make do. You don't think I'm leaving her behind to spread stories about me, do you? Now get those robes on."

The three of you quickly slip into coarse, woven robes. You notice Dr. Z's robe is a royal purple trimmed with gold braid. You and Dana must be wearing what ancient slaves wore.

"I even have an extra voice translator for your nosey friend," Dr. Z thrusts the small boxes at you, and you hang them around your necks and under your robes.

"Now, I'd like to become a trusted advisor to the powerful king of Israel, David. But I think I'll make my moves in that time before he was crowned. Take me to him!" he orders.

You pause, considering setting the dials for something else.

"No monkey business!" Zarnof warns, pointing his gun at Dana's head. He gives you specific directions for AL, and watches you type them in.

Obediently, you set AL down before a large house with lawns and trees. Servants are going in and out, busy about their work. The smell of cooking meat and spices floats on the air.

Go to page 75.

Dr. Z strides through the front portals of the house without you. As you hesitate, unsure whether or not to follow, a woman calls to you from a doorway. "Here, you! Go fetch more water at the well."

"Wait a minute, we're not—" then you shrug. You're dressed like servants. That food smells great, and servants eat, too.

You are just delivering the jugs of water to the kitchen when you spot a little boy slipping into a small room off the kitchen. You can tell by his sly movements. that he's not supposed to be there. You set your jug down and signal for Dana to follow you.

By the time you reach the door the child comes out again, clutching something in his grubby hand. You grab him by the shoulder and demand, "What have you got there?"

He starts trembling. You give him a shake and repeat your question. He slowly opens his hand to reveal a small handful of bronze coins.

Choices: You say, "Well, they can't be worth much," and let him go (turn to page 88).
You turn him over to the steward to be disciplined (go to page 97).
You decide to deal with him yourself (go to page 72).

Even after Rhoda finally lets Peter into the room, some still don't believe it's him. "Peter is dead!" "This must be his angel!" they cry.

Mark goes forward, "Is it really you, Peter?"

The large frame of the former fisherman shakes with laughter, "It is really the flesh and blood Peter! You were praying to see me, right?"

Now everyone gathers around him, talking at once. "Did Herod release you?" "How did you escape?" "What happened?"

Peter holds up his hands for silence. "Herod didn't release me, God did. An angel awakened me and told me to follow. I did—and the prison gates opened before us. In the street, the angel disappeared. Tell the others that I am free. I must get out of here before Herod learns what has happened."

Herod is sure to set up a manhunt for his escaped prisoner and to increase his persecution of the Christians now. But you'd like to hear more about Peter's miraculous escape.

Choices: You talk to Peter more (go to page 73).
You stay to help the Christians in Mary's house (go to page 89).

As soon as the words leave your mouth, you wish you hadn't interfered. The woman is looking at you strangely. "Well, your son is so hungry and people are starving everywhere," you finish lamely.

Then Elijah turns his head slowly and glares at you—or rather, straight through you. You back up right into Chris. "Let's get out of here," you say.

Back in AN, Dana says, "I felt sorry for that hungry boy, too. I wonder what became of him."

Chris says, "I think we're wasting our time waiting around here. We should look ahead for Jezebel."

**Choices: You try to see what happened to the widow and her son (go to page 82).
You move ahead in time a bit (go to page 86).**

You and some other Christians slip over Mary's balcony and through the garden to a quiet side street. Then you scatter in different directions. It is early morning, and the rising sun glistens on the white buildings of Jerusalem. You can already tell it's going to be a hot day.

"I'm not so sure we were smart to leave Mary's house without breakfast," Dana says.

You are about to suggest you go look for some food when you turn a corner and run squarely into two large men. They wear russet capes over their leather breastplates, and close-fitting bronze helmets. They draw their swords, but that wasn't really necessary. You already know they mean business.

"Here are a couple of those Christians!" they growl. You wonder how they knew who you were. Are there spies at Mary's house? The soldiers keep talking. "By the order of Herod, we are searching for one Simon Peter. He was chained to two sentries in a guarded prison, and yet he disappeared last night. You will tell us what you know of this, or you will pay for it."

"But we don't know anything!" you protest.

"Maybe some time in a prison cell will improve your memory," the guard closest to you sneers, edging his sword close to your ribs.

They march you off to Herod's Tower of Antonia.

THE END

You decide to eavesdrop around Zarnof's house to learn where—and to what time period—he's flying in AL.

"Look," Dana whispers, pointing to an open window. "A light just went on in that room. Let's sneak over there and see if we can learn anything."

Crouching behind the evergreen bushes that border the low brick building you edge closer to the window. You can hear voices distinctly from the room above you. A gravelly voice is saying, "You mean you let those guys go anyplace they wanted? What if that flying cigar doesn't get them back here?"

"They'll get back all right," says a voice you recognize as Zarnof's. "Then all that remains is for me to reprogram the chronograph and the cartograph for Europe in the 1700s. I've studied all of Napoleon's mistakes as well as his successes. I won't be defeated at Trafalgar or at Waterloo! I'll grind Nelson and Wellington into the dust! I'll be emperor of the world!"

An evil laugh jangles in your ears as you and your friends scurry back to Professor Q's. Things look worse than ever: Dr. Zarnof wants to change the world with AL—and AL is already gone!

Go to page 10.

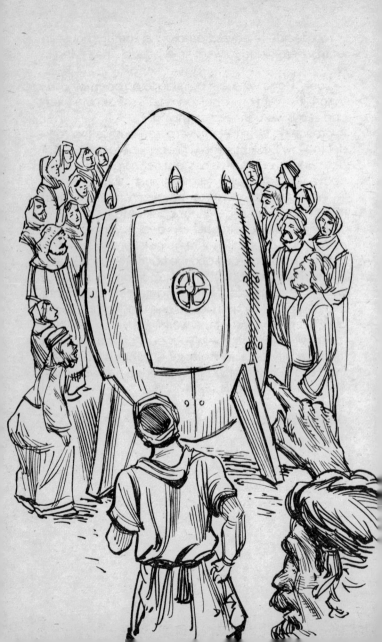

"As soon as you have made my cake, make cakes for yourself and your son," Elijah says to the widow. "The Lord God of Israel has said that your barrel of meal and your bottle of oil will not be empty throughout the famine."

The woman hurries away to her home, with Elijah following her, and you following Elijah. You don't have long to wait to see the promise come true.

"Look!" the woman cries, "I mixed enough oil and flour to make a cake for this man, but my oil bottle and flour barrel are no emptier than before. Praise be to Jehovah!"

You are just thinking how hungry the smell of baking bread is making you when your attention is distracted by commotion down the street. People are yelling and running there from all directions. Dana and Chris are in the lead, but soon you aren't far behind them.

When you round a corner, you stop abruptly and stare at the sight in front of you. AL, gleaming in the sun, is sitting right in the middle of the street. The crowd is milling around the machine, pushing it and knocking on it. Someone throws a stone that ricochets off the metal with a twang. "They're going to wreck him!" Chris cries.

Just then two heavy male voices speak up behind you. "Hey, there's the Doc!" "How'd you get here?"

Choices: You rush up and push AL's invisibility button (go to page 98).

You say, "Tell them the game's up, Dr. Z. We're going home" (turn to page 109).

82

You move ahead in AN just a few months. When you look out, you see that Elijah is still staying with the widow. But things don't seem to be going well. As you walk up to her house you hear brokenhearted screams and sobs. You follow the sounds inside. There on a little pallet is the limp form of the widow's son.

"Looks like you were right," Dana whispers. "He did starve to death."

You shake your head and point to the freshly made cakes on the table. "I don't think it was starvation. He must have gotten sick or something."

Just then Elijah comes into the room.

He walks to the grieving woman. "Give me your son," he says quietly. The mother picks up the lifeless body and places it in Elijah's arms. He turns and strides to the next room, lays the child on a bed, and kneels beside him. The door is only open a crack, but you can hear Elijah's voice. "O Lord, my God, have you brought tragedy upon this widow? Let this boy's life return to him!"

There is a pause. Nothing happens.

Elijah repeats his plea a second and third time, while you hold your breath in suspense.

And then the prophet is standing in the doorway, holding a boy with rosy cheeks and shining eyes. "See?" Elijah says. "Your son lives."

Sobbing with joy, the woman kneels at Elijah's feet, "Now I know that you are a man of God, and that your words are true."

Go to page 83.

You cough to clear the lump in your throat. Dana is unashamedly wiping tears from her eyes. Your group slips quietly out of the door. In the sunlight, even Dr. Zarnof's eyes look unaccountably red.

But Chris has his mind on something else. "If those thugs were coming here, I think we would have picked up AL's signal by now. Is there something you aren't telling us, Doc?" he demands.

You can see that Zarnof has been moved by the scene you just witnessed. "I don't know where they are," he says quietly. "But if much twentieth-century time has elapsed, they are probably home by now. I told them to be back the same night."

"That's more like it," Chris says. "What are we waiting for? Let's go!"

"Yeah," you say. "I sure hope Pat unplugged the popper, or else that popcorn's gonna be BURNT!"

THE END

"You're back!" the professor exclaims, rushing across the room to you and your friends. "You found AL? Where is he?"

You all shake your heads. "No, we just came back for something we forgot," you say, pointing to your clothes.

"Oh, my goodness, I forgot your costumes!" cries the professor and hurries over to a large closet.

In a few minutes he has you all attired in appropriate robes and sandals. "Most careless of me, most careless," he keeps saying, shaking his head as you all get back in AN and strap on your seat belts.

Go to page 64.

As you start to walk away, you see a young servant boy go up to Samson and say, "Here, I will lead you."

You don't hear any more because you walk across the crowded noisy room, looking for Zarnof. He's probably with the rulers somewhere. It's incredibly hot in the temple, and all the noise is making your head ache.

All of a sudden, the people start screeching louder than ever. You put your hands over your ears, but not before you hear a woman near you shriek, "The roof is falling!"

You look the direction she's pointing just in time to see a block of marble crashing toward you.

This is not going to help your headache!

THE END

You arrive near the top of a small mountain by the sea. The whole population of Samaria seems to be here, too, and it looks like you just missed something big. Jezebel isn't there, but Ahab is standing before Elijah, looking rather dazed. A little further on up the hill you see two altars. One has the remains of a fire smoldering on the top. The other altar has an un-burned sacrifice lying on it—and all around it are scattered bodies of men in bloodied yellow robes.

You're wondering what happened, but then Elijah's words bring good news to everybody. "Go back to your palace, King Ahab. Eat and drink your fill, for the drought is ended. I hear the sound of rain."

Rain? You can't hear anything. You look up. There's not a cloud in the clear blue sky.

Elijah calls a servant to him, and the two of them go on up the mountain. Ahab and the people are moving slowly toward town, talking over the events of the day as they go. Suddenly Elijah's servant runs back to the king. "Elijah bids you to hitch up your chariot and hurry home before the rain stops you," he urges.

Many people who hear this guffaw loudly, but Ahab puts the whip to his chariot horses.

Choices: You run (go to page 94).
You walk (go to page 90).

"Poor little kid," Dana says.

You look at him and at the pitiful handful of coins. "Well," you shrug, "they can't be worth much. And it really isn't any business of ours. Don't get caught again, kid, you might not be so lucky the next time."

The child gives you a brief smile that looks more sly than grateful, then slips away.

He has no sooner disappeared than a rough hand seizes your arm. "What are you doing by my accounting room?" a harsh voice demands.

"Nothing," you stammer, wondering if you should tell about the kid you let go.

"Nothing? You call this nothing?" The hand is now pointing to a bronze coin by your foot. "So you're the one who's been stealing my coins? I knew I'd catch you sooner or later."

"Wait a minute; it wasn't us!" you protest. "It was that little kid."

"Yeah, sure. Two weeks in a cell should give you time to think up a better story."

With no more ceremony, you and Dana are locked in a stone-walled room with straw on the floor and one tiny window. As the bolts on the door clank into place, Dana says, "On top of everything else, the little sneak stole my gold bracelet, too."

THE END

Every day you think you'll go home, but then there is so much to do to help with the work of the church and you love getting better acquainted with these people.

One day Dana comes to you with some exciting news. "I've gone to church all my life, but I never really became a Christian—till today!" she beams. "I want to go home to tell my folks."

"That's great!" you say. "Why don't you go on without me? Tell the kids at the party they can have my share of the pizza. Pick me up later; I'm going to stay here a little longer."

THE END

As you walk you glance out to sea. "Hey, there's one cloud," you note.

Chris looks in that direction. "There sure is, but it's pretty small. It'll take a while for that to work up much of a rainstorm."

The words are no sooner out of his mouth than the sky darkens and becomes swollen with clouds. Suddenly the rain falls in torrents. It is so dark and the rain so blinding you can't see where you're going. The water rushing down the mountain turns everything to slippery mud underfoot. You have no idea where your companions are. You lose your footing and feel yourself slipping down the mountain, washed along by the flooding waters. This looks like **THE END.**

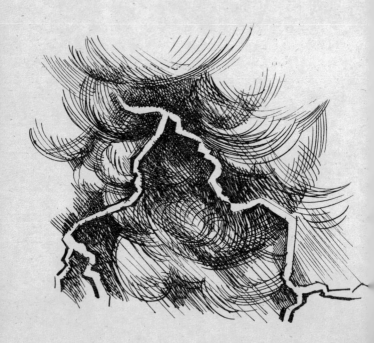

By the time AL lands you in Antioch, Dana has re- membered a little about it from her history reading. "This was the third largest city in the Roman Empire!" she exclaims as your climb out AL's door.

You don't know how big Antioch is, but it certainly is beautiful. Its white buildings cluster along a riverbank between green mountains and the blue sea. When you locate the Christian church there, you find believ- ers of many colors, from many countries. Paul, Barna- bas, and the other leaders keep quite busy with teaching and preaching. You and Dana befriend their young helper, John Mark.

One day, after a long prayer session with the church leaders, Paul and Barnabas announce that they are leaving Antioch.

"You're being kicked out?" Dana asks.

Barnabas chuckles. "No, my young friend, not at all. These good people would like us to stay forever—but they feel even more strongly that we should travel and share the good news of Christ in other cities. We'll begin by sailing to my birthplace: the island of Cyprus."

John Mark runs up to inform you that he will be sailing, too, as the apostles' assistant. "Would you like to come along?" he asks.

He doesn't need to ask twice. But Dana comes up with a more practical question. "What are we going to do about AL?" she whispers.

Choices: You say, "Let's try to smuggle him aboard" (turn to page 103)**.**
You say, "I don't know; let's pray about it" (turn to page 102)**.**

Suddenly there is a big commotion outside. Everyone rushes to the doorway to see ten young men stride across the courtyard. Before you have time to wonder what's happening, the woman directing the servants shoves a platter of meat into your hands. A basket of fig cakes is thrust at Dana. "Serve the master, and be sharp about it," she orders.

You find the master is lounging on plushy cushions in front of a long, low table, along with Dr. Zarnof and several other men, all richly robed. There are tall goblets in front of each one, and two small boys are busily filling them with a dark red liquid. From the splashes on the tablecloth, you can tell this isn't the first time they've been filled.

You are passing around your platter when the young men you had seen outside are ushered in.

Go to page 93.

"We bring a message to you from David," one of them says, bowing to the master. "He wishes you long life, Nabal, and good health."

At this, Nabal snorts, and his friends laugh.

"We have not harmed your shepherds while they were shearing near us, nor have we stolen anything," the young man continues. "We have helped protect your flocks from wolves and robbers. So we ask you to find favor with our request, and give us food for ourselves and for your servant David." The men bow again at the end of the speech.

Nabal rises unsteadily to his feet. His face is flushed an angry red. "Who is David? Shall I take my bread and water and meat and give it to these men of whom I know nothing?" He falls back heavily on his cushions. "Now begone, all of you!"

As they leave the room you hear the visitors say to each other, "There'll be trouble when David hears this."

"You're right, he won't take that rude treatment...."

Choices: You think it's smart to leave now (turn to page 112).
You see a way to stop the fight (turn to page 95).

You start running. There is only a tiny cloud on the horizon, but you aren't taking any chances. Suddenly you see a streak of dark hair and coarse robes flash by you on the way down. It's Elijah, and he even passes up Ahab's chariot!

Back in Jezreel, your whole party takes shelter in the first building you come to. Then you are horrified. "The machine!" you shout. "We left AN on the mountain.!"

Already the sky is boiling with sodden black clouds, and the rains have started.

"I'll go back for her," Chris yells over the noise of rolling thunder.

"It's too late. You'll never make it," you reply.

But soon you feel something solid and heavy bump the wall of the building. Holding on to each other so as not to get swept away in the deluge, you and Chris go out to investigate. It's AN! She rolled down the mountain right to you.

"Let's go home and dry out," Dana says, ringing the water out of her long hair. "Maybe AL's back there by now."

"Sounds good to me," you say. Even the soggy Dr. Zarnof looks like he's had enough history for a while.

THE END

Even in the short time you've been here, you've seen that although Nabal is a slob, his wife, Abigail, is as good and wise as she is beautiful. You're sure she can do something about this.

You find her in a small room near the kitchen. "Mistress, excuse me," you say, bowing. "I think you should know that David sent messengers out of the wilderness to greet our master, and Nabal insulted them." You explain what happened.

Abigail knows exactly what to do. She puts you and every other servant on the place to work. You begin gathering food from the storehouses and packing it in baskets on donkeys: two hundred loaves of bread, five roasted sheep, a hundred bunches of raisins, two hundred cakes of figs, and more.

"Go on ahead, and I will follow," Abigail orders.

Go to page 96.

You don't have very far to travel before you meet David and his men, wearing full battle attire, coming through a mountain ravine.

Abigail jumps off her donkey and falls at David's feet. "Listen, I beg of you. Pay no attention to Nabal, for he is a fool. I am to blame: I did not see the young men whom you sent. I beg of you not to shed blood needlessly or avenge yourself upon us. For the Lord will fight your battles even as you fight the battles of the Lord."

David looks kindly at her. "Blessed be the Lord for sending you here," he says. "If you hadn't come, I would have slain Nabal and all his household. Now go in peace."

As you ride back with Abigail you are thankful for her quick thinking and for David's forgiving attitude. That was a close call!

THE END

"Looks like a good chance for us to make points with the steward," you say to Dana. "Come along, you little thief."

You feel the scrawny body stiffen under your grasp, but to your surprise, the child doesn't cry.

It's easy enough to spot the steward at the far side of the kitchen. He is conferring with one of the head cooks. You stand before him for some time before he gives you his attention. "Yes?" He looks down at you as if from the top of a lofty mountain.

"I caught this kid stealing, sir," you thrust the child forward.

"Oh, it's you again, is it, Amos? Is your mother still sick?" the steward asks in his gravelly voice.

Amos nods and holds out his hand with the coins in it. The steward takes the coins. "If you try that again, you shall be thrashed, Amos." The steward turns to the assistant next to him. "I want food and healing herbs taken to his mother. We need her to work in the vineyards. In the meantime, Amos, you report to the husbandman and see what you can do to replace your mother's labor. But get something to eat first," he adds.

"And now," the steward returns his attention to you, "I don't remember hiring you two. If you've snuck in with those vagabond sheepshearers, it's time you learned your place is not in the kitchen."

He snaps his fingers and you are dragged off. "Scourge them, then send them back to the shearers," the steward commands.

Go to page 105.

98

Hoping that in the mob's frenzy no one will notice you, you reach over and flip the small switch on AL's side. Then you fade back quickly into the crowd. The object of the disturbance quickly dissolves from sight.

When you get back to your friends Dana is laughing, "Now they're really confused," she says.

"Yes, but I think I'd better get AL out of the middle of the street before some chariot comes along and crashes into him," you say.

It's good to be back inside AL again. You set the cartograph to move to a field nearby, and then look for your friends again. But as you come up to them you realize you've made a mistake. Dana and Chris have been overpowered by Dr. Z and his henchmen!

Your first impulse is to run, but then you realize you hold the upper hand. "And what do you propose to do with my friends?" you ask calmly.

"It don't matter to us none whether we silence 'em here or back home," one of the thugs says. "Just depends on how cooperative you want to be."

Go to page 99.

"And how do you think you'll get back to your lab?" you ask. "There are two invisible time machines around here somewhere. You could grope for quite a while before you find them. Unless you decide to cooperate with me, that is."

"Don't you know where the other one is, Doc?" they demand. Dr. Z. shakes his head helplessly.

"Now, suppose you untie my friends," you suggest cooly. "And, just to even the odds a bit, we'll let them tie you this time," you add when the leather thongs have been taken off Chris and Dana.

You quickly settle that you will take one thug back with you in AL, and Chris and Dana will pilot the others in the larger AN. "Shall we take them to the police station?" Chris asks.

A little grin plays around the corners of your mouth as you say, "How about the state mental hospital? I know some men in white coats who would just love to hear the stories these three guys could tell."

THE END

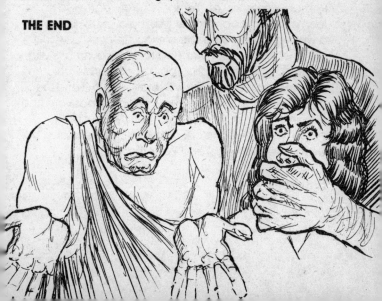

When you finally reach Cyprus you look for Paul, Barnabas, and Mark.

"There they are," yells Dana, pointing toward a ship at the dock.

You see the three men start walking toward a group of buildings. You don't want to lose them in the crowd, so you push through the people and squeeze your way past the carts, giant bundles of cloth, and smelly fishing nets.

In the city square of Paphos, capital city of Cyprus, you find the three missionaries standing in front of the Jewish synagogue. Paul is speaking and a large crowd is gathered around, listening respectfully. Mark comes over to you and explains that people listen to them because Jewish scholars are taught not to reject the opinions of any learned men without first hearing them and thinking them through for themselves.

But Mark is especially excited that Paul and Barnabas have been invited to speak to Sergius Paulus, the Roman governor of the island. You agree to meet them there later, and, after walking around Paphos for a while and admiring some exquisite copper work for sale in the bazaar, you head for the governor's villa.

As you enter through a portico of marble columns, several servants pass you with platters of fruit and meat. You'd like to follow them, but a steward stops you. "The servants' quarters are below," he says gruffly.

"Oh, I know we look like servants," you explain, "but we're here with Paul and Barnabas."

Turn to page 121.

Sitting on the waterfront at Seleucia, Antioch's seaport, you are stumped with what seems like an unanswerable problem, but you do keep asking God to help you out. Then you find you needn't have worried. Mark speaks to the ship's captain that is to take you to Cyprus, then turns to you with a look of anxiety. "There is no more room on the ship. What will we do?"

You and Dana look at each other and grin. "No problem," you say. "We'll get passage on another ship, and meet you on Cyprus."

Mark only has time for a quick slap on your back before he is hurried aboard and his ship weighs anchor.

Dana shakes her head in amazement. "You really did pray about that, didn't you?"

"Yup!" You grin at her.

Go to page 100.

"Can't you just fly AL aboard?" Dana suggests. "After all, you got him from Antioch to the seaport here."

You look at the small, overcrowded boat rocking precariously in the blue Mediterranean. "It looks pretty tricky."

"Do you suppose we could carry him between us, then?"

Dana's suggestion sounds impractical, but you haven't thought of anything better. Between the two of you, you are able to move AL about six inches. Then his smooth, egg-shaped sides slip from your fingers.

"I thought aluminum was supposed to be light," Dana says.

"Depends on how much of it there is," you reply.

"Maybe we could borrow a catapult and fling it aboard," Dana suggests with a mischievous grin.

Then you see people going up the gangplank, taking animals with them. "I've got it!" you yell. You run to a little boy who apparently has been left to mind a small donkey while his family shops at the market. "I want to rent your donkey," you say, holding out a few copper coins.

Dana shakes her head doubtfully when you return with the little animal.

"Well, they're supposed to be strong," you say.

Turn to page 104.

After much struggling and straining, you finally hoist the invisible AL onto the donkey's back. You and Dana each hold one side of AL to steady him. Going up the gangplank is the hardest part—there's not much width on that ramp to keep one or all of you from landing in the Mediterranean. You move slowly, and all seems to be going well until a small boy decides to run down the gangplank and past you to the shore. He bumps you, and you bump the donkey, and …

KERSPLASH!!

You come to the surface sputtering, and see that Dana and the donkey are doing the same thing. "Well," you admit, "I don't think this is working. It's about time I asked God for some help or ideas or something."

Soaking wet—and a few coins poorer than you started—you wade to shore, pushing the floating AL ahead of you.

Turn to page 102.

In a very short time you learn a lot about sheep-shearing. You learn that it is hard, dirty work; that sheep smell terrible; and that the whole job is a lot worse when you have to do it with a sore back from the whiplashes you were given.

But you do get to hear the gossip from the house—and what news it is! First you hear that Abigail, the mistress, has ridden off with a whole packtrain of food for David and his men, who are hiding out from King Saul. Then you hear that Nabal, her husband, has died in a drunken rage. And before the astonishment at that has died down, you hear the most amazing thing of all—David has taken Abigail to be his wife!

You are just wondering where all that leaves you, when a familiar voice yells at the head shearer. "Let my slaves go! Do you think I brought them here for your benefit?"

You never thought you'd be glad to see Dr. Zarnof, but you are.

"Nabal was a drunken fool," Zarnof says disgustedly. "Take me home. My plans need some refinement."

You nod silently, and you set AL to take you to Professor Q's. You think that what Zarnof's plan needs is confinement and Professor Q is just the man to see to it.

THE END

"Come on, Doc," you shout. "This party is going to get rough. Let's get out of here!"

But the doctor is swaying and chanting with the other revelers, fully caught up in the spirit of the thing.

Feeling really desperate, you yell again, "Come on, we've got to go!"

There's only one thing to do—you take a good hard swing at the doctor's jaw and he slumps to the floor. Dragging him to the time machine is no easy task, and he bumps hard on every step of the temple. He's going to have a great display of bruises to show for this day's adventure.

By the time you get to the ship, Dr. Z's coming around. "I said I didn't want to leave!" he shouts at you. "Take me to another party."

Go to page 47.

You look at Paul. The apostle looks angry. He holds up his hands for silence and points at Elymas. "You son of the devil! You are the enemy of everything that is good. You are full of all kinds of evil tricks. You always keep trying to turn the Lord's truths into lies! Because of this, the Lord's hand will come down on you now. You will be blind and for a time you will not see the light of day!"

For a moment everyone is silent. Then a terrible scream rends the air. "I am blind! I cannot see!" Elymas flails his arms, groping frantically, trying to find someone or something to hold on to.

You are horrified by what you have seen. In your other journeys in time, you have seen miracles. You have read about people being healed and fed and even raised from the dead in the Bible. But this seems to be just the opposite.

Dana looks ghostly pale, and her eyes are wide with alarm. "Paul cursed him, and he's blind," she says in a whisper.

Choices: You stay to talk to Paul (go to page 111).
You abandon the mission (go to page 113).

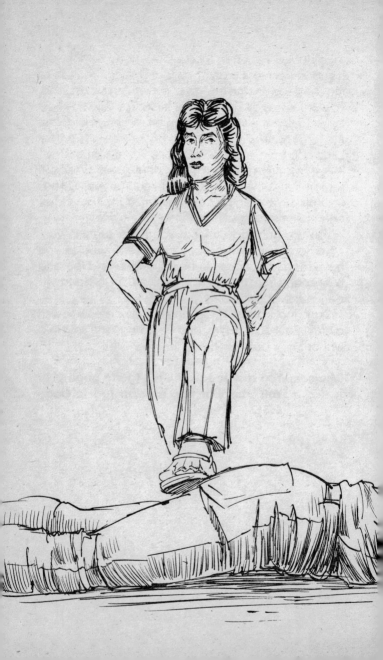

One of the thieves turns on you menacingly, "Don't be so sure. The game ain't up until I say so," he snarls.

You dodge the punch he swings at you and Dana steps into the space you left. She moves her arms quickly: a right inward block, an incredible front snap kick, a chop to the side of the crook's neck—Dana has laid him flat. You and Chris stand gaping at her.

"Anyone else want to try?" she challenges. Dr. Z and his cohort draw back. Dana relaxes and brushes herself off. "That move was called the Sword of Destruction. I told you I was an orange belt in karate, but when we get home I think I'll be ready to test for my blue."

THE END

Dr. Zarnof, in his best imitation of a visiting potentate, signals that you are his servants and not to be appropriated by Ahab or anyone else.

At first you are relieved, but this proves to be a bad situation because now, at least in the eyes of Ahab, you are in Zarnof's power.

"I think we came to the wrong place," Chris frets, pacing the floor. "There are lots of beautiful women in the Bible. What if they went to see Esther or Sarah or Rachel or Mary Magdalene or ..." he pauses, his eyes wide with dread at his next thought.

You read his mind. "Or Eve," you say.

Go to page 119.

You and Dana stand there, amazed and confused by what you have seen. Paul talks to the governor some more, then walks over to you. "You cursed Elymas, Paul!" you say, trying to make sense out of it all.

Paul places a hand on your shoulder and says solemnly, "A few days of blindness may be the only way God can get Elymas to listen to him. I know. It was that way for me. I will pray that God will make it so for Elymas. In the meantime, we could not let him block the truth. Now the governor is ready to believe."

"Then you don't hate Elymas?" you ask, still puzzled.

"Why, no!" Paul says. "I love him. So does our Lord. But sometimes God has a hard time getting our attention. Because of his opposition to the true light, Elymas will live in darkness for a while."

"How long?" Dana asks.

"That is not for me to say," Paul says rather sadly. "I spent three sightless days seeking to bring my heart and mind into conformity with God's will after I was struck blind on the road to Damascus. Every man must make his own decision whether or not to accept the Light of the World."

THE END

Dr. Z groans wretchedly. He has turned a sickly green from his overindulgence. He slowly staggers to his feet. You and Dana each take an arm and lead him reeling from the room.

"Now we can call the shots around here," you say to Dana as you buckle Zarnof in AL. Unfortunately, you forgot about his gun. "I wanna shee David," he shouts drunkenly, waving the weapon around.

The chances of his hitting you or Dana are pretty slim, you realize, but it could be just as disastrous if he shot up AL. So you decide to obey him. It's a cinch he can't be reasoned with in this state.

Go to page 26.

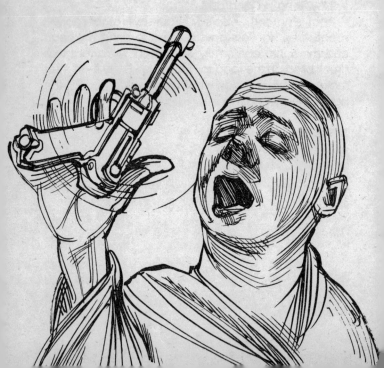

"I think it's time to go, too," you say, feeling rather upset. "I better tell Mark, so he won't worry about us."

Mark isn't as surprised by your announcement as you had expected him to be. "I'm considering leaving soon, too," he says.

"Why?" you ask.

"Well, I'm not sure I'm cut out for all this. What's more, when we left home, my cousin Barnabas was the leader. Now everything seems changed, and Paul is in charge...." He is quiet for a while. "Anyway, I'll miss you," he says with his quick, warm smile.

Even after you've been home for some time, you haven't forgotten Mark, either. You're really excited to hear the next Sunday school lesson about him.

You learn that Mark did leave the mission, and that Paul was pretty unhappy about it. When Paul and Barnabas planned another missionary journey, Barnabas wanted to take Mark again—and Paul refused, calling the young man a deserter. So Barnabas and Mark went to Cyprus, and Paul went to Greece with Silas.

But you are glad to learn that the story had a happy ending. Paul later recommended Mark highly to other Christian churches. And in the last letter the apostle wrote, he said, "Bring Mark to me, for he is profitable to me for the ministry."

THE END

You open your eyes slowly and put your hand to your aching head. Before you can speak, Dana puts a cup of cool water to your mouth.

When you look around, you can't believe it. You're back in your own home. "How'd I get here?" you ask her.

"You'd never have believed it. Dr. Zarnof ran right through all those angry people and dragged you to safety. After we brought you home, he and Chris went back to Professor Q's. The prof says that if AL is returned, he won't press charges against Zarnof."

You shake your head wonderingly. "I thought I was a goner."

"I know," Dana grins at you. "But it would have been just too much to get killed on your birthday."

"Yeah, and before I even opened my presents," you say.

THE END

Since posing as university students was Dana's idea, you tell her that she can do the talking. She pulls a notebook out of her pocket and puts on her glasses.

"You do look older with your glasses on," you say, feeling a little better.

When the door is opened, you're pleased to find out that Doctor Zarnof is short—so short he has to look up to you. The light glistens off his smooth, bald head and his round tummy protrudes from the opening of his white lab coat. The first impression he gives is of a cuddly teddy bear—until you look at his hard, glinting eyes.

"We're from the **Collegiate Gazette.** Surely you've heard of our award-winning newspaper?" Dana says in her most adult voice. "This month we're highlighting the work of the history department, and since you are, of course, the most—er—illustrious person in the department, we were hoping you'd give us an interview."

Go to page 62.

Everyone in Saul's camp seems to be in an unnaturally deep sleep. From your hillside vantage point, it isn't hard to see Saul sleeping in the center of the camp. And David and Abishai are standing over the sleeping king of Israel. His spear is stuck in the ground by his head.

"God has delivered your enemy into your hand," Abishai says softly to David. "Let me pin him to the earth with one stroke of this spear. I won't have to stab a second time!"

"No!" Even in a whisper David's voice is commanding. "Saul is God's anointed king. I will never harm him."

Zarnof mutters something, and you're afraid he'll give your presence away, but David is busy. You see him signal Abishai to take Saul's spear and the jar of water that is also near his head.

"David's a fool and a weakling!" Zarnof is saying. "He'll never have another chance like that. That God of his arranged it for him, and he was too stupid to realize it."

Choices: You think Zarnof is right (go to page 46).
You admire David's decision (go to page 56).

"Let's get out of here!" you say to Dana. "Sorcerers and magic give me the creeps!" You run all the way back to AL, and set the dials for home. Dana gives you a puzzled look, but says nothing.

Several days later, Dana approaches you, Bible in hand. "I found out what happened to Paul and Elymas," she says. "God's power struck Elymas temporarily blind, and the governor of Cyprus believed in Jesus after all."

"Wow!" you say. "I guess I didn't need to be worried. God is stronger than sorcerers. I should have known that."

"You know what else?" Dana adds. "Right after that incident, John Mark left the mission and went home. As far as Paul was concerned, Mark deserted them!"

"I wonder why?" you murmur.

"Well," shrugs Dana, "I guess we'll never know."

THE END

You and your friends agree that you'll try to find Dr. Zarnof's buddies in the Garden of Eden. And, after a slight struggle, the three of you manage to get the tubby Zarnof himself into AN.

Chris sits down at the controls. "This isn't going to be easy," he mutters. "I wish I knew this machine as well as I knew AL."

When AN finally lands, you aren't really sure she's landed. The machine keeps rocking back and forth. When you open the door and step out into the hazy twilight, you immediately sink into—water!

"Watch out!" you cry in warning, but it's too late. The other three are already in the sea with you.

"I knew this was tricky," Chris laments. "I bet we're a little early—at the time in creation when God hadn't made the dry land yet!"

"Let's get back into AN," Dana suggests. But when you turn around, you see that it's too late. Water has sloshed in AN's open door, and she's sinking fast.

"Well," you address the others glumly, "how long can you tread water?"

THE END

120

You walk casually down the street to the address in the phone book.

"At least it's not a huge place," you say. "Just a ground floor and a basement."

"All those bushes will help, too," Chris adds. "And it's getting dark. I don't think anyone on the street will see us spying. I'll explore the front."

"I'll check out the basement," Dana offers.

"Right. I'll do the back windows," you say. "Then we'll meet here again."

As noiselessly as you can, you creep toward the back of the building. Chris and Dana will have some light from the streetlights to guide them, but the back of the house is black.

There are three windows in the building's main floor. One of them is brightly lighted. You also spot a window well with a faint flicker of light glowing from the basement.

Choices:. You check the upstairs window (go to page 17).
You look down the window well (turn to page 21).

The names work like a charm. The steward apologizes, and soon other servants bring you clean robes and basins of water, and wash your feet. That tickles! All cleaned up now, you are ushered into a magnificent chamber in the villa, where Paul is apparently telling the Roman governor about Jesus. Again, Mark walks over to greet you.

Suddenly Paul's talk is interrupted by another man in the room. "Blasphemer!" the voice says. "It is written, Cursed be he who hangs on a tree! Governor, this man is calling a condemned criminal our Messiah!"

"Who's that guy?" you whisper to Mark.

"That is Elymas, a sorcerer for the governor," Mark replies. "He has opposed our message the whole time here."

**Choices: You are afraid of sorcerers, and decide to get out of there (turn to page 118).
You stick around to see what happens (turn to page 107).**